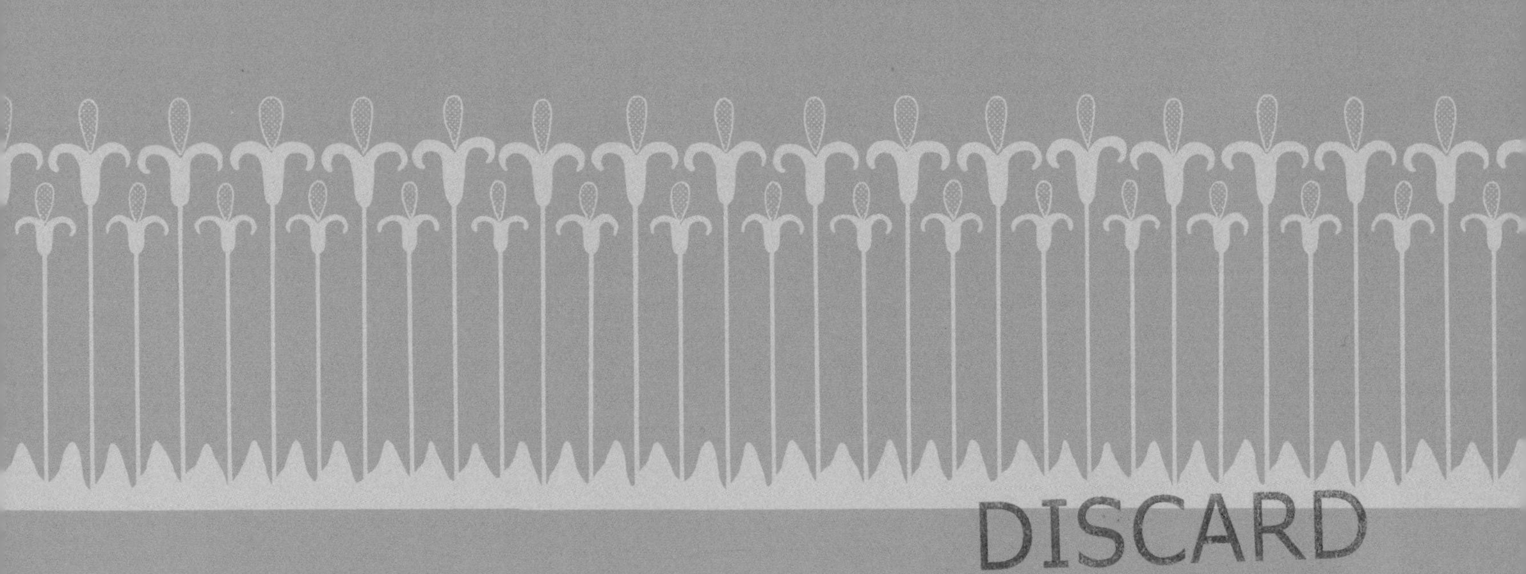

THE TOMB ROBBER AND KING TUT

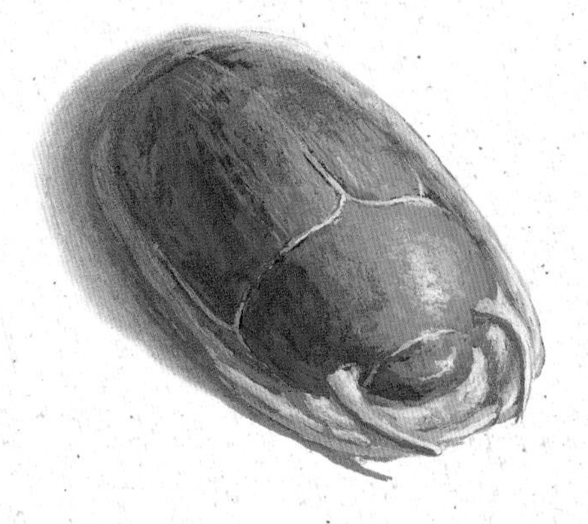

SARAH GAUCH

illustrated by

ALLEN GARNS

VIKING

An Imprint of Penguin Group (USA)

VIKING
Published by the Penguin Group
Penguin Group (USA) LLC
375 Hudson Street
New York, New York 10014

USA • Canada • UK • Ireland • Australia • New Zealand • India • South Africa • China

penguin.com
A Penguin Random House Company

First published in the United States of America by Viking, an imprint of Penguin Young Readers Group, 2015

LIBRARY OF CONGRESS CATALOGING-IN-PUBLICATION DATA
Gauch, Sarah, author.
The tomb robber and King Tut / by Sarah Gauch ; illustrated by Allen Garns.
pages cm
Summary: Hassan, grandson of tomb robbers, joins the dig of King Tut's tomb,
but must show honesty to continue working.
ISBN 978-0-670-78452-3
1. Tutankhamen, King of Egypt—Juvenile fiction. 2. Excavations (Archaeology)—Juvenile fiction.
3. Brigands and robbers—Juvenile fiction. 4. Honesty—Juvenile fiction. [1. Tutankhamen,
King of Egypt—Fiction. 2. Excavations (Archaeology)—Fiction. 3. Archaeology—Fiction.
4. Robbers and outlaws—Fiction. 5. Honesty—Fiction.] I. Garns, Allen, illustrator. II. Title.
PZ7.G2316To 2015
[E]—dc23
2014028638

Manufactured in China
1 3 5 7 9 10 8 6 4 2

Set in Caecilia Designed by Nancy Brennan
This art was created using gouache and pastel on watercolor paper.

Penguin
Random
House

To Khalil, without whom I never would have stayed
and fallen in love with Egypt and the Middle East.
And to the Gurnawis, who once had a village
between the Valley of the Kings and the Queens. —*S. G.*

To Cooper, Annie, & Cason —*A. G.*

"We've discovered a step, Mr. Howard!" the *rayyis* calls out to the man in the white hat.

There is silence as Mr. Howard approaches the foreman. My heart pounds.

The man, his eyes wide and serious, bends down. Carefully he brushes the sand from the worn rock.

Is it the step to the tomb? I want to ask. *To King Tut's tomb?*

But I don't ask these questions. Instead I turn and run down the valley, toward my father's sugarcane fields. I know he will be angry if I'm late. But I *must* get on Mr. Howard's dig!

For years Mr. Howard has come to the valley near my village where the great pharaohs, the kings of Egypt, are buried in underground tombs. And for months I've pleaded with Baba, my father, to let me work with Mr. Howard, as he searches for a certain king's tomb—King Tut's tomb.

Today I ask again. "No!" Baba replies. "We are *farmers* now."

I turn away.

"Hassan," Baba says, his voice softer now, "you are the grandson of tomb robbers. Your grandfather sold the tombs' treasures, but only when they needed wheat, seeds, a cow. Still, most people think tomb robbers are thieves who robbed out of greed. . . . Farming is honest work, Hassan. Everyone knows that." He puts a hand on my shoulder, then walks away.

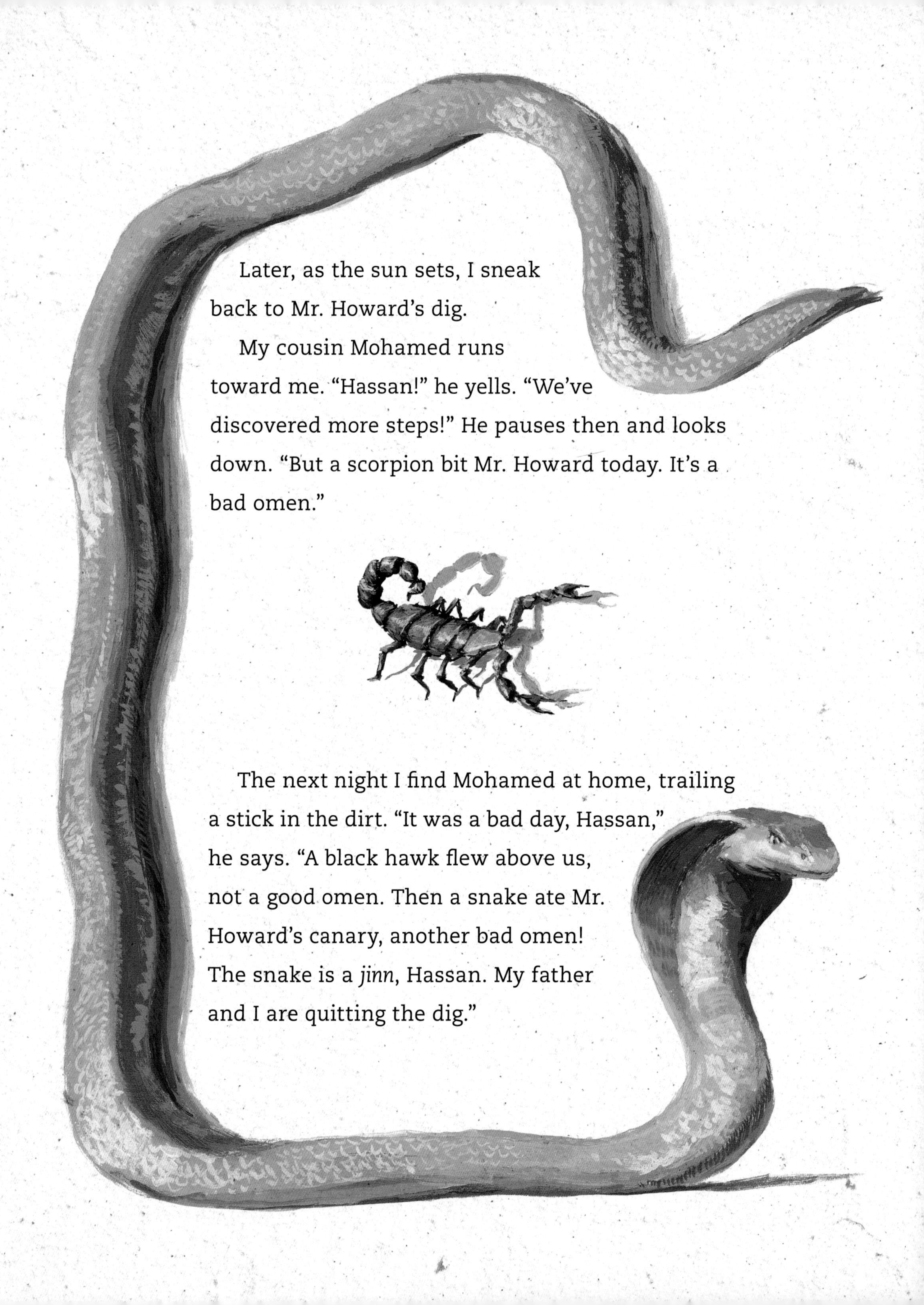

Later, as the sun sets, I sneak back to Mr. Howard's dig.

My cousin Mohamed runs toward me. "Hassan!" he yells. "We've discovered more steps!" He pauses then and looks down. "But a scorpion bit Mr. Howard today. It's a bad omen."

The next night I find Mohamed at home, trailing a stick in the dirt. "It was a bad day, Hassan," he says. "A black hawk flew above us, not a good omen. Then a snake ate Mr. Howard's canary, another bad omen! The snake is a *jinn*, Hassan. My father and I are quitting the dig."

On my way home from Mohamed's, I think of the narrow tunnels that wind from house to house, leading to the tombs. My ancestors built these tunnels many years ago in their search for treasures. I once crawled into one, even though people said they were full of *jinns*, evil spirits. No *jinns* appeared. Not one!

"Baba, they need workers on Mr. Howard's dig!" I say, bursting through the door. "Please, Baba, let me go!" I don't say anything about the omens.

"No, Hassan," my father says, frowning. "I need your help in the fields."

I bite my lip. "The dig has stopped until an English lord arrives," I explain. "He pays for Mr. Howard's dig and must come before they continue. It's two weeks, Baba," I say. "Until then I'll work twice as hard, *three* times." Baba still shakes his head no.

But I don't give up hope. The next day and the next, I rush to do chores. I collect clover to feed the donkey. I get Baba food for lunch. I work hard all day, until the sun sets behind the mountain.

Finally it's the night before the dig begins again.

"Baba, the English lord has come," I say, my stomach knotted as camel rope. "Mohamed says he'll do my field chores. Please, can I work on the dig?"

Baba sits, thinking a long time. Finally he looks up and nods. "All right, Hassan," he says, "you can go. You've worked hard . . . but remember, you're the grandson of tomb robbers. Show that you're honest, that you won't steal."

"I will show them," I say solemnly, but my heart is racing!

The next morning, I dress quickly and run after the other men and boys going to the dig.

The *rayyis* stands on a ledge, his arms across his chest, like a pharaoh. "Tomb robber!" he says, glowering at me. "Get to work!"

I know I am here only because many workers have left. I know if I don't work hard and show that I'm honest, I won't be allowed back. I hoist a heavy load of sand onto my shoulders like the other basket boys.

But where is Mr. Howard? I wonder.

Suddenly, there is a shadow in the brightening sky, a man with a white, brimmed hat. Mr. Howard! And next to him, an elderly man with a walking stick. The English lord. And beside him, a lady in a feathered hat.

That day we uncover the first step, and then another, descending lower and lower. Sweat pours down my shoulders. Finally we have sixteen steps uncovered.

"A doorway!" someone yells. "Plastered shut!"

"And, look, with seals!" the *rayyis* says.

Mr. Howard hurries over to examine them. "King Tut's seals."

Clearing the rubble away basket by basket, we unblock the doorway. Behind it is a passage, wide as the stairs and taller than a man.

The passage is almost empty now. We are resting when the *rayyis* points to me. "Tomb robber," he says, "go down and get the last of the rubble."

Slowly I descend the sixteen steps. Kneeling on the ground, I shovel the last rubble into my basket. My hands are raw and my back aches. That's when I see it. A stone of blues and greens, framed in gold and shaped like a beetle! It's heavy and beautiful, and very old. I look at the treasure for a moment, and then I hear footsteps. I swivel around and quickly hand the scarab to the *rayyis*. The man's fierce eyes and his frowning face slowly soften into a wide smile. I hide my own grin and turn back to work, less tired now.

Mr. Howard and the English lord join us in the dark passage. Suddenly the *rayyis* gasps, pointing excitedly. "*Bab*, another door."

It is a door! And with pharaonic letters, a jackal, and four seals—the very same seals as the first doorway!

"King Tut's seals!" the *rayyis* whispers.

What's behind it? I wonder. *Anything? Nothing?*

Mr. Howard uses a small knife to slowly chip away at a corner of the door. He makes a hole, just large enough to peer in. Then he inserts a candle, flickering wildly like a *jinn*. He looks into the hole. There is silence. The hot smell of wax. The shuffle of feet.

Finally Mr. Howard turns around, his face bright. He speaks words I cannot understand. But he looks like a man on the grandest day of his life, like Baba after harvesting his first crop of sugarcane.

The English lord and the lady in the feathered hat peer in and then back away to talk in whispers. *What is it?* I pray they'll let me see what's beyond the door. The *rayyis* looks into the hole. When he finally turns around, he smiles. "King Tut's tomb!" he says. "Intact!"

He motions me to the doorway. I put my eye to the hole.

"*Yalla*, let's go!" the *rayyis* says. But I rise on my tiptoes and see something between the guarding statues—*another door! What more could there be?*

The *rayyis* pulls me away and we head up the long passageway. "Tomorrow," he whispers, "Mr. Howard will want as few workers as possible, to avoid stealing." My heart plummets, like a bucket dropping in a well. *But what about the new door?* I think. *I have to come back!*

Up top, Mr. Howard and the *rayyis* stand talking. Then the *rayyis*, still like a pharaoh, points to the basket boys and other workers he wants tomorrow. "You, you, you."

I can barely see him.

Finally the *rayyis* stops in front of me. He uncrosses his arms. "You too, Hassan," he says, "tomorrow."

I feel my face break into a wide grin. Even I, Hassan, grandson of tomb robbers, will return tomorrow. Even I will see what's behind the next door.

I walk home, tired and happy. Baba will be proud.

The sun is setting in a centuries-old sky, a sky older than the pharaohs—older than King Tut.

AUTHOR'S NOTE

When Tutankhamun became pharaoh of Egypt in 1333 BC, he was only eight or nine years old and ruled Egypt until his death at around seventeen years. Compared to the other great pharaohs of ancient Egypt, Tutankhamun, the child king, was relatively insignificant. In fact, not long after his death he was virtually forgotten. Rubble from other tombs in the Valley of the Kings buried his tomb, and a few years later, clearly not knowing what lay underneath, the pharaohs built workers' huts over the tomb's entrance.

And this is how it remained until Howard Carter returned for his last season in the Valley of the Kings in late 1922. Carter, a stubborn but rigorous and well-respected archaeologist from Britain, had spent five years clearing the Valley down to the bedrock. A clay cup, gold foil, and clay seals with Tut's name on them helped convince Carter that Tut's tomb existed somewhere in the Valley, despite the naysayers, who claimed all the Valley's ancient treasures had been found.

Then on November 26, 1922, Carter discovered Tut's tomb and its magnificent treasures that mesmerized the world. Even though Hassan's story is largely based on the author's imagination, a boy like Hassan *could* have been there when Carter peeked through that hole into the Antechamber, the first room he discovered, full of shimmering gold couches with lion and hippo heads, a golden throne, and statues of guards, gold serpents curling from their foreheads. Tut's couches, chairs, even chariots, all just the way they were the day Tut was buried, more than 3,000 years before.

Carter went on to discover three more rooms full of amazing finds, including four gilded wooden shrines, one inside the other. Inside the fourth shrine, he found a stone sarcophagus with three mummiform coffins. And inside the third coffin of solid gold, King Tut's mummy—the first royal mummy to be discovered undamaged by tomb robbers—its head covered by a spectacular solid gold death mask.

Maybe there was a young boy like Hassan to see all this. We know Hassan's village of tomb robbers was a real village, Gurna on Luxor's West Bank. In 2007, the Egyptian government demolished Gurna in order to excavate the pharaonic Tombs of the Nobles that lay underneath. After years of pleading with the government to preserve their village and allow them to stay, the Gurnawis were forced to resettle elsewhere.

The workers' fear of a bad omen or curse may also have been true. Several people who saw Tut's tomb soon after it was discovered died, including the dig's benefactor, Lord Carnarvon, the English lord of this story, who died of pneumonia just months after the tomb's discovery.

The village of Gurna, Egypt, before it was demolished in 2007